DRACULA AND BEYOND
Famous Vampires & Werewolves in Literature and Film

THE MAKING OF A MONSTER

Vampires & Werewolves

DRACULA AND BEYOND

Famous Vampires & Werewolves in Literature and Film

by Shaina Carmel Indovino

Mason Crest Publishers

MASON CREST PUBLISHERS INC.
370 Reed Road
Broomall, Pennsylvania 19008
(866)MCP-BOOK (toll free)
www.masoncrest.com

First Printing
9 8 7 6 5 4 3 2 1

Library of Congress Cataloging-in-Publication Data
Indovino, Shaina Carmel.
  Dracula and beyond : famous vampires & werewolves in literature and film
/ by Shaina Carmel Indovino.
       p. cm.
  Includes bibliographical references and index.

ISBN 978-1-4222-1803-7
ISBN (series) 978-1-4222-1801-3
Paperback ISBN: 978-1-4222-1956-0
Paperback ISBN (series) 978-1-4222-1954-6

  1. Vampire films—History and criticism—Juvenile literature. 2. Werewolves in motion pictures—Juvenile literature. 3. Vampires in literature—Juvenile literature. 4. Werewolves in literature—Juvenile literature. 5. Horror tales, American—History and criticism—Juvenile literature. I. Title.
  PN1995.9.V3153 2011
  791.43'675—dc22
                                        2010020684

Produced by Harding House Publishing Service, Inc.
www.hardinghousepages.com
Interior design by MK Bassett-Harvey.
Cover design by Torque Advertising + Design.
Printed in the USA by Bang Printing.

CONTENTS

chapter 1
THE ROOTS OF VAMPIRE AND WEREWOLF STORIES

Remember Little Red Riding Hood? An innocent little girl on her way to Grandma's house encounters a wolf. She safely avoids him, but her grandmother is later eaten and needs to be cut free of the wolf's body with a woodsman's axe.

What is the larger lesson we learn from this? Don't trust strangers. Also, don't trust wolves.

Once upon a time, there were good reasons for parents to warn their children about wolves. And then as today, parents had equally good reasons to warn their children about strangers. Stories were a good way to impress on young minds the reality of the world's dangers.

And the really good stories stuck in the human mind. They continued to be handed down from generation to generation.

Transforming a Monster into a Human

Monsters that were both human and animal were often the ingredients for those "really good stories," the ones that sent a pleasurable chill running up and down the listeners' spines. Vampires and werewolves were creatures of folklore and legend. Their stories were told around fires for centuries before they were ever written down.

When actual stories began to be written about these two creatures, the authors played on the human fear of the unknown. Stories of vampires and werewolves haunted members of high society with the threat of infiltration by vile creatures passing among them undetected. These authors created intelligent vampires and werewolves, evil that was more fascinating for being sophisticated—and for being more like us.

The classic "high-society" vampire is never detected until it's too late, and he is always shown as merciless. He is the evil that walks among humanity, cloaked in darkness, the side of human nature we dare not face. Meanwhile, the werewolf has no control over his bloodthirsty violence. He represents humanity's internal conflict between good and evil, between our spiritual nature and our animal nature. Within the werewolf's shaggy breast, however, evil always wins.

These stories served as warnings to society: Look out for these creatures, and stay away! Kill them if you must!

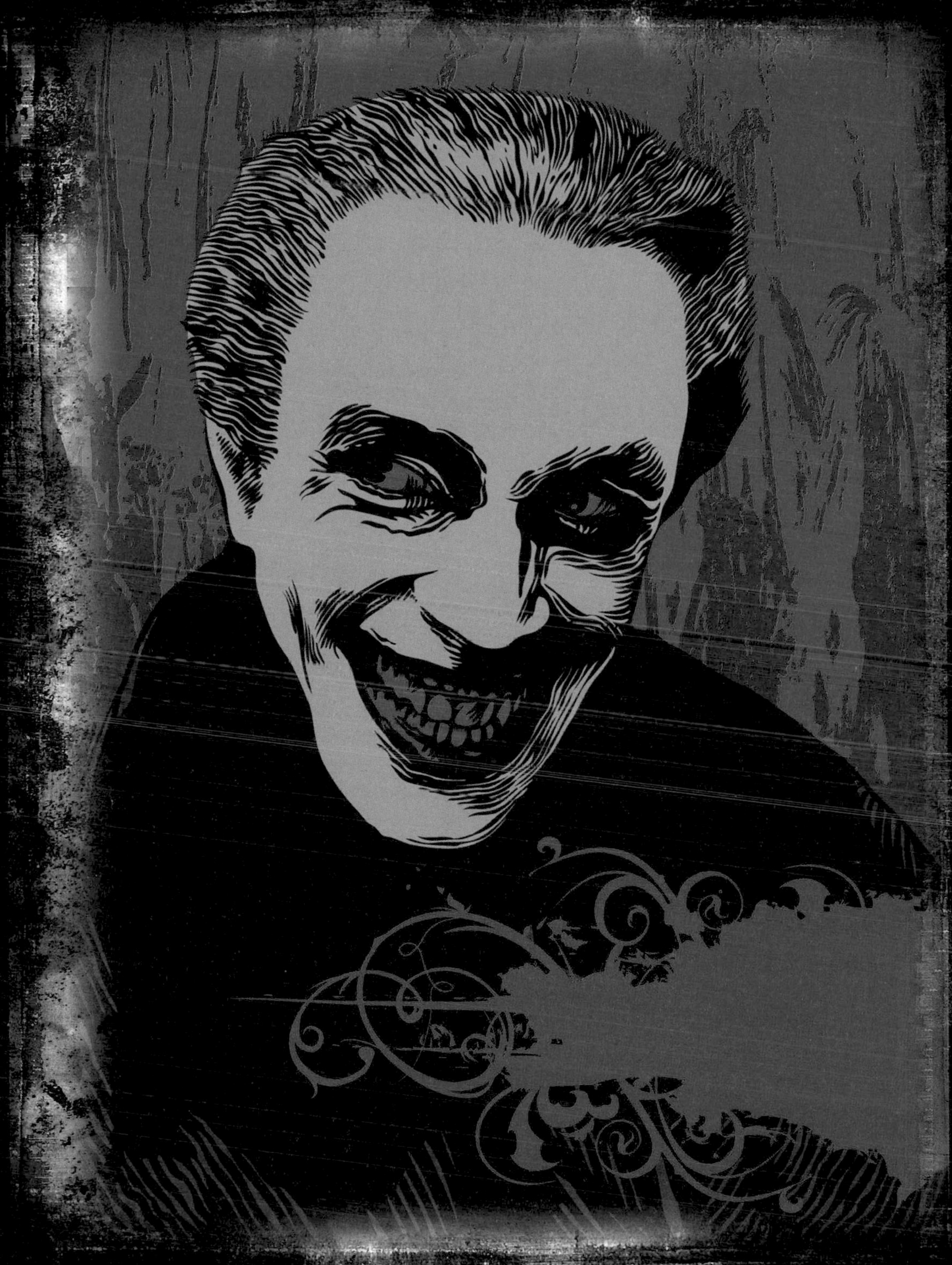

But whatever you do—do not befriend them! You will only regret it. If the vampire and werewolf represented a side of human nature, then it was a side humans refused to accept. The only answer for it was to destroy it, by whatever magical means possible.

In the twentieth century, however, the stories began to change. The story of the vampire and werewolf were now told from the perspective of an author who actually cared about how the monsters thought and felt. These authors saw a hint of goodness within the darkness. Vampires and werewolves in the new stories fell in love with their prey, and with each other. We came to understand their tormented existence, and now, we started to see them as much as victims as were their prey.

As we entered the twenty-first century, vampires' and werewolves' fascination grew, and we were entertained with new stories, both in book form, on television, and on the big screen. We learned that not every vampire wants to drink human blood. In fact, some survive on synthesized blood or animal blood—or no blood at all. Some kill themselves rather than live out their lives in loneliness and secrecy, separated from humanity. Some fall in love with humans, but restrain themselves when they get too close, afraid they might hurt the one thing they hold most dear. We also learned that some werewolves have control over their transformations, and that they are not merely trapped in one form or the other. We discovered that werewolves aren't always born that way, but that they are turned into this strange life form.

Most important, we came to understand that not all werewolves are evil, and that some of them seek to protect the Earth and even live among humans.

Somewhere along the way, we learned that vampires and werewolves are just as capable of having their own complex societies as we are. We began to take for granted that they were also capable of having family, friends, and romance—and experiencing love, sorrow, and heartbreak. We found that forbidden love could even spring to life between a vampire and a werewolf, offering us a new, dark version of the Romeo-and-Juliet story.

Finally, we came full circle: we accepted that vampires and werewolves might be just like ourselves. This time around, though, we realized that good and evil can seldom be totally separated as we once believed. If we shoot the wolf with a silver bullet, if we drive a stake through the vampire's heart, then we also destroy a part of ourselves—and we will be diminished.

When Fantasy Seems Real

Included in this book are some of the world's most famous vampires and werewolves, the ones whose stories have become a part of all our imaginations. Some you may recognize by only their names, but you will probably know at least a part of their stories. Either way, these creatures of dark fantasy have become a part of our world.

They *cannot* be ignored.

chapter 2
THE NINETEENTH CENTURY
THE GOTHIC MOVEMENT

The nineteenth century was the era when vampires stepped boldly out of folklore into literature. At the end of the previous century, in 1764, an English author named Horace Walpole wrote *The Castle of Otranto*—and invented a new literary genre: the Gothic.

Gothic fiction creates a pleasing sense of fear in its readers. It feeds extreme emotions: the sick thrill of terror alongside the chilly awe we feel in the presence of the supernatural. Gothic literature is filled with haunted ruins, moldering in shadowy spider webs. It glorifies the inevitable decay of all human endeavors by describing the delicious horror of dark secrets, madness, hereditary curses, and death.

Vampires and werewolves were right at home in this setting. One of the first Gothic stories to feature a vampire was "The Vampyre" by John Polidori, written in 1819. The idea of blood-sucking monsters was not new to the people of England, but Polidori took it to a whole new level of terror.

The Vampyre

Lord Ruthven is sophisticated, intelligent, irresistible to the ladies—and an unstoppable vampire. Perhaps his most horrifying aspect is the fact that he can so easily hide his true identity. This made him much more fascinating to readers than the brainless zombie-like "creatures of the night" that came before him.

As the story opens, Aubrey, a young and idealistic aristocrat, meets Lord Ruthven in England, where the two decide to travel together. Aubrey immediately notices that everyone Lord Ruthven meets adores him; men respect him and women swoon over him. He is described as a beautiful and graceful figure except for a few small flaws: his face is expressionless, his skin is pale, and his cheeks never blush. He seems indifferent to everything and everyone he meets, and yet not one person suspects that he might be a killer.

While the two are traveling, Aubrey receives a letter from his guardians back home, warning him that Lord Ruthven is dangerous, that he only brings pain and

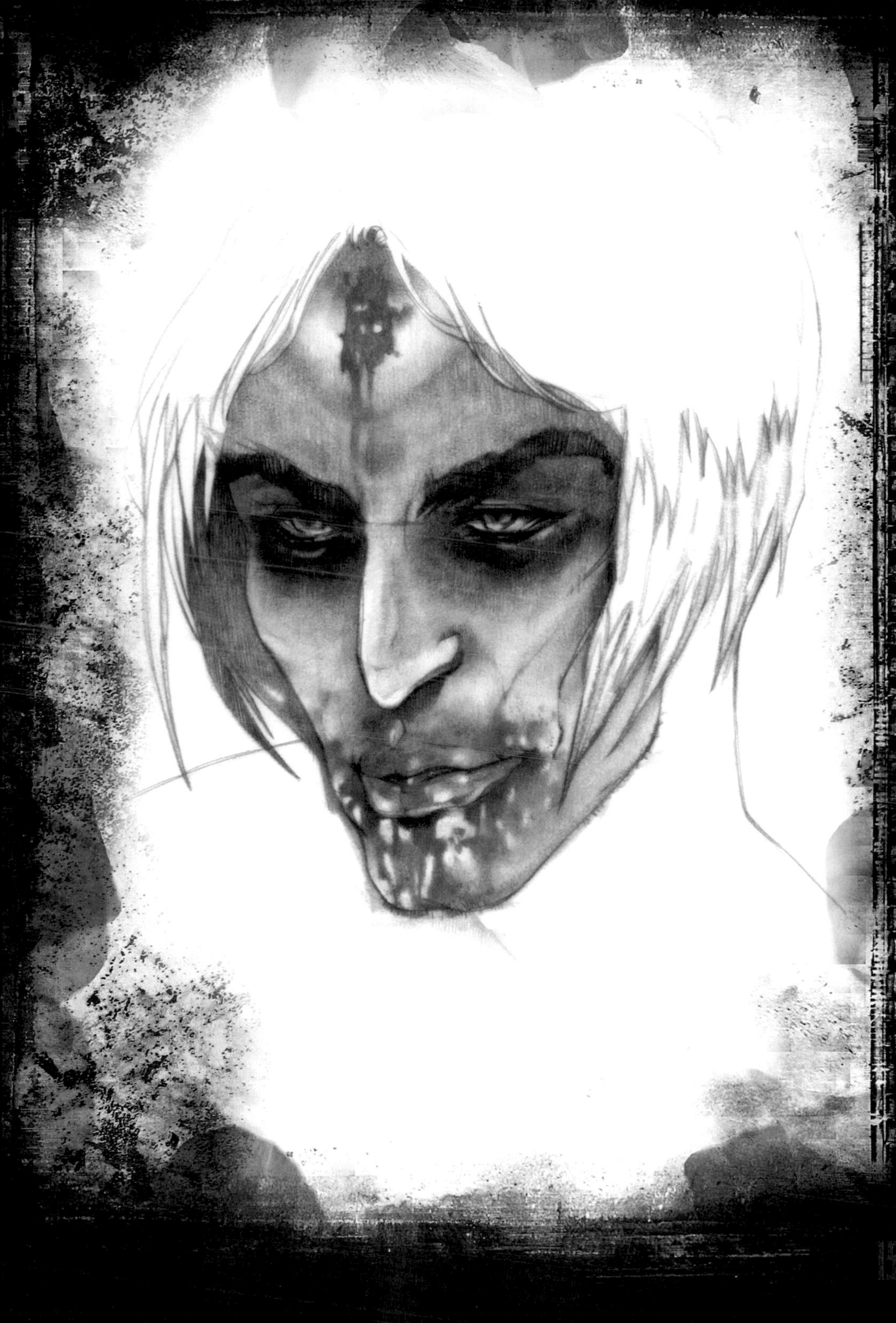

tragedy to those he meets. Aubrey obeys their warning and leaves Lord Ruthven to travel on his own.

Aubrey then journeys to Athens, where he meets Ianthe, the most beautiful woman he has ever seen. One day, she tells him about vampires: how they are able to pass through society without being detected, and how they prey on the living for months before anyone suspects a thing. Aubrey tries to convince Ianthe that these evil creatures couldn't possibly exist, but in the back of his mind, he realizes that her description of vampires might explain what Lord Ruthven is and why he is so dangerous.

Later, when Aubrey's work requires that he travel to a certain area of the woods, Ianthe and the townsfolk warn him not to stay there past dark because vampires are known to lurk there. Unfortunately, he loses track of time, and he becomes lost in the dark woods while a thunderstorm rages overhead. His horse takes off in a panic, carrying him even deeper into an area of the woods he does not recognize. Soon after, he is attacked by what he can only assume is a vampire, but the villagers scare the monster off with their torches, and he is saved. Ianthe, however, is killed in the chaos. The only marks on her body are two puncture wounds on her throat: the bite of a vampire.

When Aubrey encounters Lord Ruthven again soon after, Aubrey is convinced that he is the monster that killed Ianthe. However, Lord Ruthven manages to regain

Aubrey's trust, and they travel on together to other areas of Greece, not heeding the warnings that bandits may find them.

Bandits do in fact attack the companions, and Lord Ruthven is seriously wounded. With his dying breath, Lord Ruthven commands Aubrey not to reveal any knowledge he has about him or his death for at least one year and a day. Aubrey agrees, and Lord Ruthven

dies. The next morning, Aubrey discovers that his body has disappeared.

Attempting to put all of this behind him, Aubrey returns to England. There, to his amazement, he finds Lord Ruthven, alive and well, courting Aubrey's sister. "Remember your oath!" Lord Ruthven whispers to him.

Aubrey keeps his promise, but it ultimately drives him mad. Then he learns that his sister plans to marry Lord Ruthven—and their wedding day will be exactly one year since the day that Aubrey saw Lord Ruthven die. Aubrey is still bound by his oath, but in desperation, he writes a letter to his sister, begging her not to marry Lord Ruthven until the day when Aubrey can at last reveal the truth.

Aubrey is dismissed as insane, however, and the guards do not deliver his letter to his sister. When a year and a day have finally passed, Aubrey reveals everything he knows about Lord Ruthven, that he is a manipulative monster that must be stopped. The guards try to find him, but it is too late: Lord Ruthven is gone, and Aubrey's beloved sister is his latest victim.

In this story, the vampire takes advantage of Aubrey's innocence and virtue. He uses Aubrey's idealism and integrity to manipulate him so that Aubrey loses everything he values in himself: his love for Ianthe, his grip on reality, and his ability to protect his sister.

"The Vampyre" set the stage for the vampire stories that followed it. Lord Ruthven's dark shadow still falls across the world.

Carmilla

Why do we often see vampires as male? Can't they be female?

Of course! When Joseph Le Fanu wrote "Carmilla" in 1872, he proved that female vampires could be just as terrifying as male. Carmilla even had some qualities of a werewolf. (Or, perhaps we should say, a werecat!)

As a young girl, Laura dreams of a beautiful lady who visits her room and bites her, but leaves no mark. Then, when Laura is a teenager, a carriage accident brings a young girl by the name of Carmilla to her family's home. Laura and Carmilla discover that they share the same dream of the beautiful woman, and this draws them together.

Carmilla's mother must leave on an urgent trip, and so she leaves Carmilla in the care of Laura's family. Almost immediately, Carmilla begins doing some strange things. She makes several romantic advances toward Laura, and she also seems to sleep most of the day, while she sleepwalks at night. Laura doesn't know what to think of her. When Laura sings a religious song, Carmilla is repulsed.

And then, an ancient portrait painted several hundred years ago is delivered to the house, a portrait of a long-ago ancestress, Mircalla, Countess Karnstein. The portrait doesn't just resemble Carmilla; it looks like her *exactly*, right down to the mole on her neck.

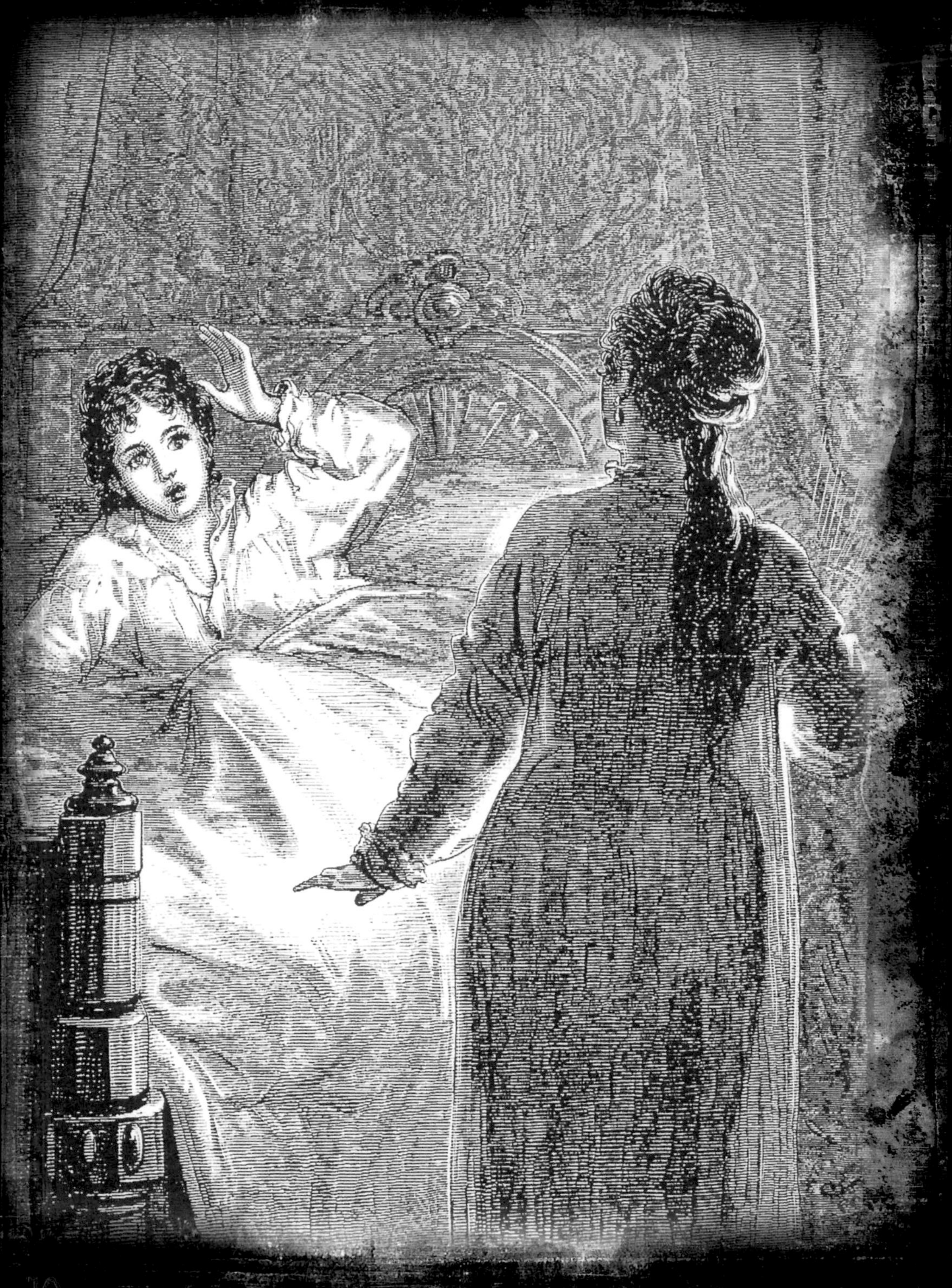

Soon after this, Laura has dreams of being bitten on the chest in the middle of the night by a cat-like creature. Her health slowly declines. A doctor visits and says she should never be left unattended.

Laura and her father decide to travel to Karnstein, to search for the home of their ancestress, the mysterious Mircalla. On their journey, they encounter a general who tells them a story that sounds very familiar. When the general was taking care of his niece, he says, a mysterious woman and her daughter came to them. The woman asked if she could leave her daughter, Millarca, in his care, as she had urgent business. He agreed, and soon after, his niece began showing the exact same symptoms Laura had. A priest told the general that the girl was likely a vampire, so the general hid in a closet in his niece's room and waited to confront the beast. When he saw a cat-like creature slink in and begin to bite his niece's neck, he drew his sword and attacked. The creature turned into Millarca and fled, unharmed. His niece died immediately.

The general then travels with Laura and her father to search for the tomb of Millarca, the Countess of Karnstein, but a woodsman tells them that the hero who drove the vampires out of the region moved the tomb. While the general and Laura wait together in a ruined chapel, Carmilla appears to them. The general is furious at the sight of her, for he realizes that Carmilla and Millarca and Mircalla are all the same person. The letters in their names are simply rearranged.

He attacks her with his axe. (Just as the woodsman attacked the wolf in Little Red Riding Hood!) At this point, a descendant of the long-ago hero shows up, and he is able to find Carmilla's (Mircalla's) tomb. They exhume her body and destroy it, putting an end to the terror she has caused.

As in Polidori's "Vampyre," Carmilla slips into the proper lives of her prey, bringing with her corruption and death. The nineteenth century had no understanding or tolerance for lesbianism, and so they relegated this form of "unnatural love" to the dark, mysterious world of vampires, a world that seduced even as it destroyed.

Dracula

Describe what a typical vampire looks like. Say the first things that come to your mind!

If you're like most people, at the top of your list will be a dark, bat-like cape and fang-like teeth in a pale face. These characteristics belong to Count Dracula, the most famous of all literary vampires. Dracula has left his image everywhere, from cartoons to Halloween costumes to Sesame Street (remember the Count?). But where did Dracula come from in the beginning?

From the creative brain of Bram Stoker, the author of *Dracula*.

The novel starts when a young lawyer named Jonathan Harker visits Count Dracula at his castle in Transylvania in order to provide the Count with legal advice. When Jonathan learns he cannot leave the castle, he tries to escape despite being warned by the Count not to leave his room after dark. Three women, all beautiful in a ghastly way, approach him, and he falls into a trance-like state as one of the women moves closer, her lips drawn back to bite his neck.

Count Dracula storms in, however, and breaks Jonathan's trance as he forbids the woman to feed on him that night. Jonathan does not fully understand what Dracula means, but he is terrified throughout the rest of his stay. Eventually, he finds a way to escape and return back home.

But he cannot leave Count Dracula behind so easily. Ominous happenings indicate that Dracula has left his home in Transylvania. A Russian ship runs aground on the shores of England during a fierce tempest—but when rescuers go onboard, they find that all the crew are missing, and the captain's body is tied to the ship's helm. The captain's log tells of strange events that took place during the ship's journey, leading to the gradual disappearance of the entire crew. An animal

Where's Transylvania?

Transylvania is a real place. It was a part of what is today the country of Romania in Eastern Europe.

described as a large dog is also seen on the ship before leaping ashore. The ship's cargo is silver sand and boxes of soil from Transylvania.

Lucy, a friend of Jonathan's fiancée, comes down with a mysterious illness, and Dr. Abraham Van Helsing is called in to diagnose the problem. Although Van Helsing suspects Lucy may have fallen prey to a vampire, he doesn't mention it for fear that people will not believe him. Instead, Van Helsing gives her blood transfusions, fighting for her life, but despites all his efforts, she dies when a wolf attacks her.

Soon after her burial, reports circulate that some children have disappeared, while others have come home with bite marks on their necks. When their mothers ask where they've been, the children explain they have been with a beautiful woman who lured them into following her.

Van Helsing knows the woman must be Lucy. She has become a vampire, and she is now feeding on the children. He reveals what he knows to Jonathan, and they decide she must be stopped by any means possible. Van Helsing describes the way to kill a vampire: cut off her head, fill her mouth with garlic, and drive a stake through her heart.

Van Helsing and Jonathan are able to destroy Lucy, but next, Dracula turns his attention to Jonathan's fiancée, Mina. The vampire feeds on her several times, and then he creates a spiritual bond between them by having her drink some of his own blood. This telepathic connection,

THE REAL-LIFE DRACULA

Although **Dracula** is a work of fiction, a few historical facts inspired its author, Bram Stoker. Vlad III, Dracula of Wallachia in Transylvania, lived during the fifteenth century and during his reign he was known as "Vlad the Impaler." Vlad is said to have killed from 40,000 to 100,000 European civilians (political rivals, criminals, and anyone else he considered "useless to humanity"), as well as another 100,000 Ottoman Turks. His favorite method of murder was to impale people on a sharp pole (thus his nickname). Vlad III was not all bad, though; Romanians also revered him as a folk hero because he drove off the invading Turks. The name Dracula means "Son of the Dragon." (Maybe that's where he got his bat-like wings.)

however, proves to be his downfall, for Van Helsing and his helpers are able to use Mina to track Dracula's movements. They manage to follow Dracula back to his castle, where they pierce his throat and heart, ending his reign of terror that reached across all of Europe.

Dracula is a vampire, perhaps the most famous vampire in the world—but like Carmilla, he is also a shape-shifter, a man who can appear as an animal (in his case, as a wolf). Clearly, vampires and werewolves share common roots deep within humanity's dark imagination.

The Wolf Leader

Based on a folktale the original author apparently heard as a child, *The Wolf Leader* was translated into English just after the start of the twentieth century. In this story, the main character is shown to descend into misfortune because of a deal he makes with a wolf.

The story starts with a shoemaker by the name of Thibault being beaten for interrupting a man's hunting. Shortly after, he encounters a wolf walking on its hind legs. The wolf offers Thibault the chance to get revenge by exchanging a hair for a wish, as many times as he wants. Thibault agrees and soon realizes that in addition to his wishes, he is also able to control the wolves of the area. This causes people to believe he may be a werewolf.

Although his wishes do come true, he also pays a price: every single time he makes a wish, he is also wounded in some way, too. Every hair he gives up becomes long, red, stiff, and incapable of being cut. By the end of the story, only one of his hairs retains its original color. He eventually finds himself trapped in his house while the villagers burn it down, because they believe him to be a werewolf. He manages to escape, but he is banished to the woods, where he lives with the wolves and hunts the hunters who hunt them.

His life is changed forever by his pact with the wolf, and as a result, he is forced to live a life secluded in nature with his animal brethren. Nature and human society are not compatible in this story!

Dr. Jekyll and Mr. Hyde

Like *The Wolf Leader*, this story is suspiciously similar to a "deal with the devil" gone wrong (as they always do!). The story has two main characters: Mr. Hyde, a hideous man accused of trampling and assaulting multiple people, and Dr. Jekyll, a respectable doctor who has some relationship with Hyde. They are technically the same person, but we don't find that out until much later.

Mr. Utterson, a man who decides to investigate this curiosity, eventually meets Hyde and retrieves his address. As it turns out, Hyde lives in small shack attached to Jekyll's property. However, Jekyll tells Utterson not bother with Hyde.

After a year, Hyde is seen beating another person to death. When Utterson confronts Jekyll on the matter, saying that he thinks Hyde committed the murder, Jekyll apparently cuts all ties with Hyde. The two men find a note from Hyde, apologizing to Jekyll for the trouble he

An early 20th-Century movie version of Dr. Jekyll and Mr. Hyde.

has caused and saying goodbye. However, they notice his handwriting is suspiciously similar to Jekyll's.

Although everything seems perfectly fine for a while after that, Jekyll eventually starts acting incredibly anti-social and finally locks himself in his laboratory and refuses to come out. When people try to get him to leave, they make the startling discovery that the voice coming from behind the door sounds nothing like Jekyll. Utterson then breaks into Jekyll's room and realizes that the person inside is not Jekyll, but Hyde in Jekyll's clothing—and he is dead by suicide.

Dr. Jekyll admits in a letter to Utterson that he found a way to separate his good side from his bad. He created a potion that could turn him into Mr. Hyde, the infamous and hideous man that kills people without a second thought. He said turning into Hyde made him feel morally free, because when he was Hyde, he didn't care about anything he did wrong. Unfortunately, the potion did not completely separate his impulses. As Jekyll, he still had the urge to become Hyde from time to time.

He became horrified with himself after a while, and decided to stop using the potion that would make him become Hyde. His transformations eventually became involuntary, however, and he could no longer safely hide his double-identity. He returned home to his laboratory, where he locked himself inside and faced the realization that he would soon become Hyde permanently. The only way to stop Hyde was to kill him. His letter ends with a goodbye.

Although Mr. Hyde is not actually a werewolf, the fact that Dr. Jekyll finds himself involuntarily turning into a beast-like monster makes him very similar to one. Like Mr. Hyde, the werewolf represented the dark animal side of human nature. Robert Louis Stevenson, the author of *Dr. Jekyll and Mr. Hyde*, explored the battle between good and evil that goes on inside human nature and implied that once we begin to give into the "beast" within us, we will lose control of it. Eventually, it will consume all that is good in us, and we will become no better than a wild animal.

Nature as Evil

For centuries, society viewed nature as an enemy, a threatening force against which humanity must do constant battle. At the same time, humans projected their own evil tendencies onto nature. Nature might be intriguing, but it was also the antithesis of all that was good and orderly and "civilized." Stories where human beings were transformed into animals that fed on blood—whether they were cats or wolves or bats—acted as metaphors for the deep fear and loathing (and fascination!) people felt toward their secret sinful natures, the greedy, selfish part of themselves where they were all-too willing to "eat" another's life.

This outlook remained true in the nineteenth century and continued into the twentieth—but slowly it began to change.

chapter 3
THE TWENTIETH CENTURY FROM BOOKS TO THE MOVIES

As soon as film had sound, *Dracula* was adapted for the big screen. The first film stuck pretty closely to Bram Stoker's novel, with one major exception: sunlight was portrayed in the film as being deadly to vampires, leading to the later assumption that sunlight could be used to kill a vampire. This first film set the stage for what we still think of when we think of a vampire.

Have you ever seen a kid pouncing around at Halloween in a Dracula costume, proclaiming, "I vant . . . to suckkk . . . your bludd?" That line—and accent—came directly from the original movie. The actor, Bela Lugosi, had a natural accent, which accounted for his odd way of speaking.

As for the cape that's still part of every good Dracula costume, it was mentioned in the novel, but it was an important part of Dracula's costume in the movie. The vampire used it to not only shield himself from objects such as crucifixes, but also to cover his victims as he leaned in for the bite—which he NEVER did on camera. He couldn't: the cinema at the time was so censored that a scene showing something as erotic and violent as a bite on the neck would have never been allowed on the big screen.

Dracula and His Whole Family

When actor Bela Lugosi refused to work on any more Dracula films, Universal Studios had to find another way to continue Dracula's story without him. Why not Dracula's family? Many films came out as a result (too many to describe here—but if you want to know what happens in the long and drawn-out saga of the Dracula family, you should watch them!).

The second movie, *Daughter of Dracula*, begins a few moments after *Dracula* ends. Our hero from the original story, Van Helsing, is taken by the police to Scotland Yard, where he explains that although he destroyed

THE VAMPIRE BAT THAT LIVES ON HUMAN BLOOD!
DRACULA
Starring
BELA LUGOSI
A Realart RE-RELEASE

Count Dracula, it cannot be considered murder, since the count had already been dead for more than five hundred years. Instead of hiring a lawyer, Van Helsing enlists the aid of a psychiatrist, Dr. Jeffrey Garth.

Meanwhile, Dracula's daughter, Countess Marya Zaleska, with the aid of her manservant, Sandor, steals Dracula's body from Scotland Yard and burns it, hoping to break the curse that has turned her into a vampire. However, Marya's thirst for blood cannot be quenched. She resumes her hunting, mesmerizing her victims with her jeweled ring.

CARL LAEMMLE
Presents

DRACULA'S DAUGHTER

A UNIVERSAL Picture

WHY DON'T VAMPIRES HAVE REFLECTIONS?

When Dr. Garth visits Marya's apartment, he notices that she has no mirrors. This is later explained by Van Helsing, who says that vampires do not have reflections. This belief has also carried over to today, all thanks to whoever wrote the screenplay for *Daughter of Dracula*.

After a chance meeting with Dr. Garth at a party, Marya asks for his help with her little problem. Dr. Garth believes that vampirism is a psychological rather than physical problem, and so the doctor advises her to defeat her cravings by confronting them. Marya is filled with hope.

However, while Marya is painting a young girl named Lili, she succumbs to her blood lust and bites Lili. The girl ultimately dies, and at last, Dr. Garth realizes the true nature of Marya's problem.

Marya lures Dr. Garth to Transylvania by kidnapping Janet, the woman he loves. There, Marya intends to transform the doctor into a vampire to be her eternal companion. Dr. Garth agrees to exchange his life for Janet's, but before he can be transformed, Sandor, the servant, shoots his mistress through the heart with an arrow.

In *Daughter of Dracula*, the viewer for the first time feels sympathy for the vampire. Poor Marya wants so badly to be freed from her evil nature, and yet is unable to be healed. We might even feel sorry when she is killed . . . well, almost!

Werewolves Evolve on the Big Screen

In the early days of movies, few werewolves found their way onto the big screen. Once they did, however, the genre exploded. Finally, vampires had a rival! Oddly, this

THE AUTUMN MOON

Gwen recites a prophecy soon after meeting Larry, which continues to be referenced in many pieces of werewolf fiction to this day. The prophecy is, "Even a man who is pure in heart and says his prayers by night, may become a wolf when the wolfsbane blooms and the autumn moon is bright."

rivalry for popularity in the movie world parallels the rivalry vampires and werewolves feel for each other *within* that fiction! What was once an aspect of a single monster—the beast-like human who preyed on blood—now became two separate species of monsters.

The Wolf Man

Most of our notions about werewolves today can be traced back to a movie called *The Wolf Man*, released in 1941. After all, this was one of the first movies where a werewolf finally had a starring role of its own. Like many stories that would follow, the monster of this film develops a forbidden relationship with a female heroine, Gwen. However, when they first meet, Larry is not yet a werewolf. He buys a walking stick with a silver pentagram on top of it from her store. As he is leaving, Gwen explains that the symbol is a symbol werewolves see on the hand of their next victim.

As Gwen and Larry are walking together that night, they hear the howl of a wolf and a woman's screams in the distance. Larry rushes to the rescue and kills the monster with his silver-headed stick—but he is bitten in the process.

When Larry realizes that he is a werewolf, he runs to Gwen's house and tries to tell her that he must leave at once. She offers to go with him, but he refuses, trying to protect her as best he can—by staying as far as possible away from her. He retreats back to his castle, where his father explains that he has to face his fear and fight his inner evil. Larry, as a werewolf, finds Gwen and pounces on her. His father arrives on the scene and bludgeons the beast with the silver-headed walking stick. He watches in horror as his son transforms back into a human and dies.

American Werewolf in London

Arguably one of the most popular werewolf movies, this film drew heavily from its predecessor of forty years, *The Wolf Man*.

Two men from America arrive in London for a vacation, where a werewolf attacks them. One of them is killed, while the other is merely injured A villager appears and kills the werewolf, transforming its body into that of a human.

David, the surviving American, awakes in a hospital. He is visited by his dead friend, Jack, who explains that David must kill himself to end the werewolf's reign. If he does not, he will turn into a werewolf too. A nurse at the hospital by the name of Alex offers to let him stay with her, but he warns her that he must be a werewolf, and he believes that a werewolf can only be killed by one who loves it (like Larry was killed by his father in the earlier movie).

While Alex is working one night, David experiences the excruciating pain of transforming into a werewolf. After discovering that he must be responsible for several murders, David runs away to try and kill himself . . . but can't. The police eventually corner him. Alex arrives and tells him he will soon be released from this prison

Together at Last

Return of the Vampire, a 1944 film by Columbia pictures, was the first story to feature vampires and werewolves together. In this movie, Armand, a vampire, has a werewolf servant, Andreas. Armand is portrayed as evil, while Andreas is seen as a helpless victim in bondage to the vampire.

through death, and that she loves him. He is quiet for a moment, but then leaps toward her and is killed by a round of bullets from the police. When he dies, he transforms back into his human form.

The New World of Vampires

When did vampires start struggling with their humanity? When did vampires start questioning their right to drink another person's blood? When did they start feeling depressed because they will remain essentially the same while the world constantly changes around them? Or that they won't be able to tell anyone who they really are and will live their entire un-life utterly alone? All of these questions surfaced when Anne Rice released her first novel of the Vampire Chronicles, *Interview with the Vampire*, in 1976.

The main character, Louis, tells his story to a reporter. He relates how, in the deepest of depressions after his brother's death, he gave himself to "the dark gift," allowing a vampire to drink all of his blood and then drinking some of the vampire's in return. His body died a violent death, but he returned a vampire.

Louis recounts all of the long years, the people he has killed for survival. He describes his initial refusal to drink human blood, and says that at first, he survived off of rats and other small animals. He mentions a little girl that became a vampire, Claudia, who was his com-

THE NOVEL STEPS ONTO THE SCREEN

Anne Rice's *Interview with the Vampire* and *Queen of the Damned* were adapted for film, kick-starting an explosion of many more vampire-themed movies made specifically for the big screen. *Interview with the Vampire* features Tom Cruise, Brad Pitt, Antonio Banderas, and Kirsten Dunst toward the beginning of their careers. Kirsten Dunst was only twelve at the time and received three awards for her performance as Claudia. *Queen of the Damned* stars Aaliyah and Stuart Townsend.

panion for many years, a six-year-old girl who could never grow up. He curses the vampire responsible for both his dark life and Claudia's, the vampire they have searched for together and tried to kill, the vampire who is perhaps the most well-known vampire of Anne Rice's series: Lestat.

Lestat is much older than Louis in vampire-years, and he has had more time to contemplate the meaninglessness of his existence. The next few books follow his story where he, among many other things, searched for the roots of vampirism.

Lestat's popularity lies perhaps in eternal loneliness, combined with the mixture of good and evil that lives side by side within him. Is he a monster—or is he a tormented human? Anne Rice laid the foundations for

The movie **Underworld** was considered so similar to one of White Wolf's novels that the company decided to sue, claiming that **Underworld** had stolen its plot directly from their novel, **The Love of Monsters.**

a new flood of vampire stories—but these vampires were more like us than ever before. Despite their fangs and their unquenchable thirst for blood, we identified with them.

The Entertainment Industry and Vampires

Vampires and werewolves had now fully arrived on the modern-day scene. People wanted more—and several different areas of the entertainment industry fed this insatiable hunger for . . . monsters!

White Wolf's World of Darkness

Remember Dungeons and Dragons? The fantasy-themed role-playing game continues to entertain both children and adults. Several other role-playing games have been created in the wake of D&D's popularity—and some of them are built around the dark world of vampires and werewolves.

In the late twentieth century, White Wolf, Inc. created the most popular of these, an entire world based on the dark horror of vampires, werewolves, and many other dark creatures of the night. White Wolf did not stop at what we already know about vampires and werewolves, however. It went steps further to completely explain any question anyone might have ever had about the origins of monsters' history, anatomy, or social struc-ture. The story world White Wolf built starts with the dawn of time and progresses to our modern-day world, constantly updating its story to include recent events.

All the earlier vampires and werewolves were included in their story, from Carmilla to Anne Rice's Lestat. Because vampires and werewolves could seem so different from one story to the next, White Wolf created the concept of clans and bloodlines, where each clan specializes in a certain area of vampire and werewolf power.

Also described in White Wolf's huge array of game books, novels, and other published works are the origins of a deep and bitter feud between vampires and were-wolves. The hatred between the two species of monsters would play a role in the next generation of stories.

A World of Slayers

Buffy the Vampire Slayer

In the 1990s, the vampire lore of old took on new life in this movie-turned-hit-TV-show. The main character, a teen-age girl who attends school like everyone else, is given the task of destroying vampires, soulless creatures who are unworthy of life. She is equipped with a stake and crucifix, which she carries everywhere, including to school.

These are not sympathetic vampires; they are por-trayed as monstrous and merciless, killing their victims without a second thought. Whenever they are about to bite a victim, vampires transform into something more

suitable for the monster they are: their face changes shape, and their forehead bulges outward. The viewers root for Buffy, the female underdog in an action-oriented plot.

But amid the evil is Angel, the one good vampire. He rejects human blood, fights other vampires, and wishes he could live a normal, human life. As any girl who grew up when this show was popular might tell you, Angel was simply irresistible. No one could blame Buffy for falling in love with him. For the first time, we explored the concept of what it might mean to love a vampire.

Blade

At the end of the twentieth century, another vampire character arrived on the scene, with a story that would be told in three separate movies and was eventually

turned into a TV series. Blade is half-human, half vampire, and he fights his vampire cousins across the big and small screens.

Blade introduced several other new ideas to the vampire world. Before Buffy, most vampire movies showed vampires as traditional and manipulative like Dracula, rather than combative and action-oriented. Blade took what Buffy started and brought it one step further, introducing guns and hand-to-hand combat to the mix. Vampire films were no longer purely horror; now they were action movies.

In the world of Blade, the vampires are also extremely organized, a characteristic pulled from White Wolf's World of Darkness. In the long-ago days before the printed word, long before the motion picture industry or the invention of the television, stories about vampires and werewolves slowly evolved, each building on what had gone before, the story becoming more detailed, as humans developed a fuller picture of these monsters. That same process continues today, with each new book or movie building on what has gone before to create the twenty-first-century vampire and werewolf.

Born from the Comics

Blade's story was actually first created by Marvel Comics in the 1970s. The character also had a minor role in the 1970s film, Tomb of Dracula.

chapter 4

THE TWENTY-FIRST CENTURY THE TRANSFORMATION OF THE MONSTERS

Vampires and werewolves are apparently here to stay. In the twenty-first century, they have taken on new, more vivid roles in our imagination. They are no longer the terrifying evil that haunts our nightmares, though. Instead, we are fascinated with them. We think they're sexy.

True Blood

True Blood follows the lives of humans and vampires knowingly living within the same community. The

EXPOSING THE RIVALRY

Vampires and werewolves just can't seem to get along. But do you know why? Well, pick your poison: Is it because of an ancient rivalry? Is it because the vampires enslave the werewolves and the werewolves refuse to "go quietly"? Is it because the werewolves see vampires for what they really are—bloodsucking monsters—and feel the need to protect the world? The explanations keep on growing, with each one more interesting than the one before it.

vampires survive on synthetic blood created by scientists, making them no real danger to the community—theoretically. The main character, Sookie, is capable of reading minds, and falls in love with a man whose mind she cannot read, a vampire. The conservative Louisiana town where she lives experiences a string of strange murders, and Sookie becomes immersed in the world of vampires.

So why is this show the most popular HBO series since *The Sopranos*? Maybe because its storyline is full of metaphors for modern realities to which many of us relate. Vampires are the outcasts in this show, shunned by the "normal" members of society. Many of the tensions that arise between the vampires and the humans can be compared to real-life issues between gays and straights, Christians and Muslims, Mexican immigrants and Americans. Take a moral dilemma like this but remove it to fantasy world where we can deal with it more comfortably, then throw in a bit of action, drama, mystery, and romance—and you've got yourself a successful series!

Underworld

In 2003, the first *Underworld* movie added a new element to the vampire-werewolf equation: a forbidden love affair between vampires and werewolves. Selene, the main character, is a vampire. She spends her entire unlife as a "death dealer," a vampire who kills Lycans, werewolves—and then she falls in love with a man who becomes a werewolf.

In this world, vampires and werewolves are not supernatural creatures but the victims of a virus. Long ago, two brothers were bitten by different carriers of this virus: one was bitten by a bat, one by a wolf. Centuries ago, the Vampires enslaved the Lycans, using them as slaves to be the guardians of their lairs during the daylight hours, but the Lycans revolted during the Middle Ages. Ever since then, the two strains have been at war. The story continues to develop through three movies, with a fourth one planned for 2011.

Van Helsing

Remember the vampire slayer from *Dracula*? In 2004, he came back—but he looked a lot like Hugh Jackman this time!

In Bram Stoker's story, Van Helsing's first name was Abraham, but in this movie it's Gabriel. The writer/director/producer, Stephen Sommers, did not feel that "Abraham"

was an appropriate name for an action hero—and besides, Universal wanted copyright privileges to the character. The story implies that Gabriel Van Helsing is actually the Archangel Gabriel in human form. As a man, Gabriel hunts monsters for the Catholic Church, and he is sent to Transylvania to kill Count Dracula.

When he arrives, Dracula tells Gabriel they have already met; in fact, they have quite a history together. At the movie's climax, Dracula reveals that it was Gabriel who killed him—but Dracula made a bargain with the devil and become a vampire. This ironic twist makes Gabriel Van Helsing the inadvertent creator of his own archnemesis!

When it comes to the dark history of the supernatural, this movie has it all: vampires, werewolves, the Brides of Dracula. Even the monster Frankenstein has a role to play.

Twilight

Start with a story showcasing the most recent literary changes among vampires and werewolves. Then add some details that make the main characters slightly different from all vampires and werewolves in literature before them (like the fact that vampires' skin sparkles in sunlight instead of bursting into flame). Mix in a generous portion of teen romance—and you have a book series that is just as popular as the Harry Potter series for very similar reasons. Then, generate enough popularity to have a film produced from the story—and you are golden!

Vampires and werewolves have changed author Stephanie Meyer's life. The stories of Edward, Bella, and Jacob bring together a new mix of vampire, human, and werewolf. They've changed the lives of thousands of teenage girls as well, whose heads are now filled with romantic fantasies of werewolves and vampires. The dark monsters of the nineteenth century have come a long, long way.

Bestsellers

As of March 2010, the Twilight series had sold over 100 million copies worldwide, with translations into at least 38 different languages around the globe. The four Twilight books have spent over 235 weeks on the New York Times Best Seller list.

Stephanie Meyer claims, however, that she did not set out to write about vampires and werewolves. Instead, she wanted to describe the tensions faced by ordinary teenagers. Some of the series' themes include sexual purity, as well as choice and free will. She says that the books are centered around Bella's choice to choose her life on her own, and the vampires' choices to abstain from killing rather than follow their temptations. "I really think that's the underlying metaphor of my vampires," Meyer said in an interview. "It doesn't matter where you're stuck in life or what you think you have to do;

THE FOGGY NORTHWEST, HOME TO VAMPIRES

You'd think that vampires would have a hard time mixing in at a high school when their skin glitters every time sunlight falls on it. But that's why Meyer chose Washington State as the setting for her story—because of the large amount of annual rainfall and cloud cover.

you can always choose something else. There's always a different path."

The Twilight vampires and werewolves build on the stories and movies of the past, but they also create their own, brand-new world. These supernatural creatures are no longer symbols for the struggle between good and evil within the human soul, the inevitable, irresistible power of our "dark side." Instead, they have become metaphors for moral choice.

Who knows where they will travel next within the human imagination? All we can be sure of is that they will remain firmly lodged within our fantasies, creatures who in some way help us understand ourselves a little better.

WORDS YOU MAY NOT KNOW

abstain: To hold yourself back from something, keep from doing something.

aristocrat: A member of the nobility or ruling class.

classic: Traditional, typical, used as a model or standard.

conservative: Traditional, avoiding showiness; preferring to keep things the way they are and avoiding change.

corruption: Contamination, decay, made morally evil.

erotic: Related to or stirring up sexual desire.

exhume: Dig up something that has been buried, such as a dead body.

genre: A kind or type; especially has to do with a category of books, movies, music, or other works of art.

idealistic: Having high standards and believing these standards can be met; seeking out the good, excellent, and perfect.

implied: Something that is suggested without being said openly.

inevitable: Unable to be avoided.

infiltration: Entering an area or mixing with a group without being detected or noticed, with the intent to gain information or do harm.

insatiable: Unable to be satisfied.

intriguing: Fascinating; arousing curiosity.

irresistible: Having an overwhelming attraction; unable to be withstood.

lore: The body of knowledge on a particular subject, especially in terms of knowledge not studied or collected by professionals or academics.

manipulative: Controlling and using situations and people for one's own advantage.

mesmerize: Hypnotize, enchant, hold under a spell.

metaphors: Symbols; images, characters, and words used to show a relationship between two things showing how they are similar.

predecessor: Something or someone who came before and is followed by another.

seduced: Led astray; distracted away from one's purpose or values.

sophisticated: Educated, knowledgeable, experienced, and refined.

synthesized: Artificial; created and designed rather than natural.

trance: A half conscious state or daze, such as when one has been hypnotized.

transformation: A change from one thing into another.

Find Out More on the Internet

Project Gutenburg www.gutenberg.org: Includes copies of public domain literature, such as; "The Vampyre," "Carmilla," *Dracula, The Wolf Leader, Dr. Jekyll and Mr. Hyde*, etc.

Famous Vampires
vampires.monstrous.com/famous_vampires.htm.

Famous Werewolves
werewolves.monstrous.com/famous_werewolves.html.

Further Reading

Beresford, Matthew. *From Demons to Dracula: The Creation of the Modern Vampire Myth*. London, U.K.: Reaktion Books, 2008.

Brown, Nathan Robert. *The Complete Idiot's Guide to Werewolves*. New York: Alpha Books, 2009.

Curran, Bob. *Werewolves: A Field Guide to Shapeshifters, Lycanthropes, and Man-Beasts*. Pompton Plains, N.J.: New Page Books, 2009.

Godfrey, Linda S. *Mysteries, Legends, and Unexplained Phenomena: Werewolves*. New York: Checkmark Books, 2008.

Guiley, Rosemary Ellen. *The Encyclopedia of Vampires, Werewolves, and Other Monsters*. New York: Checkmark Books, 2004.

Guiley, Rosemary Ellen. *Mysteries, Legends, and Unexplained Phenomena: Vampires*. New York: Chelsea House, 2008.

Karg, Barb, Arjean Smith, and Rick Sutherland. *The Everything Vampire Book: From Vlad the Impaler to the vampire Lestat—A History of Vampires in Literature, Film, and Legend*. Avon, Mass.: Adams Media, 2009.

Bibliography

Answers.com, "Dr. Jekyll and Mr. Hyde," www.answers.com/topic/dr-jekyll-and-mr-hyde-novel-1 (6 May 2010).

Cadytech.com, "The Wolf Leader," www.cadytech.com/dumas/work.php?key=244 (6 May 2010).

Gelder, Ken. *Reading the Vampire*. London, UK: Routledge, 2006.

Izzard, Jon. *Werewolves*. London, UK: Spruce, 2009.

Kane, Tim. *The Changing Vampire of Film and Television: a Critical Study of the Growth of a Genre*. Jefferson, N.C.: McFarland & Company, 2006.

Montague, Charlotte. *Vampires from Dracula to Twilight: the Complete Guide to Vampire Mythology*. New York: Chartwell, 2010.

"The Wolf Leader." Wikipedia, the Free Encyclopedia. (6 May 2010). en.wikipedia.org/wiki/The_Wolf_Leader.

Index

Shaina Carmel Indovino is a writer living in Miami, Florida. She attended the State University of New York at Binghamton, where she earned degrees in both sociology and English. She enjoyed the opportunity to apply both her areas of study to a topic that fascinates her: the living undead!

Picture Credits